Look and Find®

Disney
PRINCESS

Dream Big Princess

we make books come alive®

pi kids Phoenix International Publications, Inc.

Chicago • London • New York • Hamburg • Mexico City • Paris • Sydney

Tonight, floating lanterns will fill the sky with light, and, for the first time, Rapunzel will be a part of it. Her lifelong dream is about to come true! Inside a village shop, Rapunzel feasts her eyes on lanterns of all shapes and sizes.

Before the sun sets, find these lovely lights:

Jasmine loves to explore Agrabah. The market is one of her favorite places to visit because she always finds something unexpected. Today she has ventured down a corridor she has never been before. What will she find?

Look around with Jasmine for these new discoveries:

this rug

this basket

bronze tray

animal figurines

lantern

this book

this vase

lute

Shhhh. **Pocahontas** is listening. She is tracking an animal that got into her village's supply of corn. The trail is not the only thing she is following. By helping her people, **Pocahontas** is also following her heart.

Help Pocahontas pick up the trail that the corn thief left behind:

paw prints

this partially eaten corncob

fur

scratched bark

broken branch

Meeko

Ariel dreams of walking on land. She loves to explore sunken ships to learn about life above…but this ship is different. A coral reef is growing over it, transforming it into a part of her world. *Do people on land dream about living under the sea?* Ariel wonders.

Float around and find Ariel's under-the-sea neighbors:

 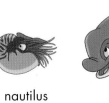   

turtle   nautilus   dolphin   shrimp   shark   sea horse   ray   this crab

Tiana's dream was to open Tiana's Palace. Now she keeps her dream alive—and keeps customers coming back—by trying new recipes and using the freshest produce. The best way to get fresh fruits and vegetables is to grow them herself…on the roof of her restaurant!

Roll up your sleeves and pick these gumbo ingredients:

celery

garlic

tomatoes

onions

bell peppers

jalapeños

okra

Mulan may not love practicing calligraphy, but she loves and respects her family. She also loves and respects the person her family raised her to be! To stay true to herself, Mulan practices sword fighting, archery, martial arts, horseback riding, and strategizing…along with brushwork.

As Mushu tries to help, search around for these important implements:

 saddle   staff    rope    map   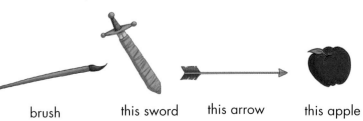 brush   this sword   this arrow   this apple

Cinderella waltzes across the dance floor, enjoying the music and the company at her royal ball. She wants all the guests to enjoy themselves, so she has made special accommodations for the tiniest of her friends. It just wouldn't be a ball without them!

While the dancers count their steps, look for Cinderella's animal companions:

Jaq · Luke · Mary · Suzy · Bert · Gus · Perla · Mert

Belle spends hours in the castle library dreaming and reading about adventures and far-off places. But today, Belle is choosing books to donate to the village library. She wants everyone to have the chance to look through these windows to the world!

While Belle and her friends pick out books, look around the library for these worldly stories:

The Pretend Prince

Provincial Perils

the Sword and the Swashbuckler

DARING DAMSELS

The Magic Hat Rack

Gwendolyn's Travels

Float back to the lantern shop and find 20 suns that are as golden as Rapunzel's magical hair.

What else is waiting to be discovered in the marketplace? Adventure back to Agrabah with Jasmine and seek out these magic lamps:

Trek back to the forest with Pocahontas and search for these other animals:

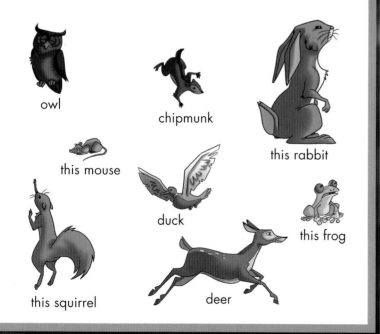

owl

chipmunk

this rabbit

this mouse

duck

this frog

this squirrel

deer

Swim back to the sunken ship with Ariel and find these objects transformed by the reef:

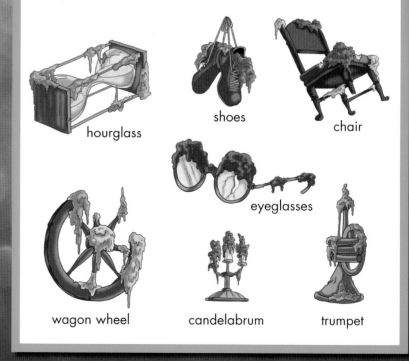

hourglass

shoes

chair

eyeglasses

wagon wheel

candelabrum

trumpet

Put on your gloves and go back to Tiana's garden to help her find these tools:

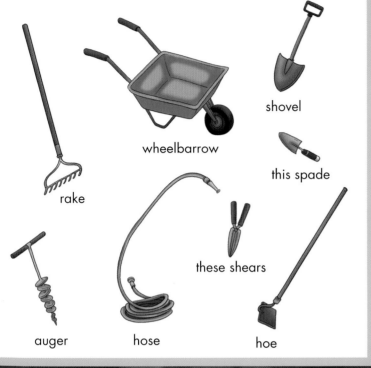

wheelbarrow

shovel

this spade

rake

these shears

auger

hose

hoe

Just like people, flowers are unique. Ride back to Mulan's practice and spot these one-of-a-kind magnolia blossoms:

Dance back to the ball and find these tiny touches Cinderella left for her furry friends:

cheese plate

this chair

ice sculpture

ROYAL MOUSE BALL

banner

punch bowl

candle

bouquet

Not all the treasures in the castle library are books! Page back to Belle's book donation and look for these precious pieces from around the world:

Spanish painting

German cuckoo clock

Persian rug

Chinese scroll

Greek bust

Egyptian pyramid

British armor